D1200829

For Kathy & for Liz —R.R.

For Felicity, my amazing agent, who is brilliant at untangling problems —Z.H.

Thank you to our editor, Sue Buswell, and designer, Beccy Garrill

 Published in the United States by Rodale Kids, an imprint of Random House Children's Books,
a division of Penguin Random House LLC, New York. Originally published in slightly different form in the United Kingdom
by Andersen Press Ltd., London, in 2020.
Rodale and the colophon are registered trademarks and Rodale Kids is a trademark of Penguin Random House LLC.
Visit us on the Web! rhcbooks.com
Educators and librarians, for a variety of teaching tools, visit us at RHTeachersLibrarians.com
Library of Congress Cataloging-in-Publication Data is available upon request.
ISBN 978-0-593-17317-6 (trade) — ISBN 978-0-593-17318-3 (ebook)
MANUFACTURED IN CHINA
10 9 8 7 6 5 4 3 2 1
First American Edition

The Problem with PROBLEMS

by RACHEL ROONEY

illustrated by ZEHRA HICKS

Rodale Kids New York

Problems are creatures.

They come in all sizes—from tiny to huge.

Some wearing disguises.

Knotty . . .

Hairy . . .

Slippery . . .

Tough . . .

Sticky like superglue, gathering stuff.

Each one is different—I've met quite a few.
But all of them want to make trouble for you.

They like to set traps.

They'll stand in
your way.

They turn the sky cloudy and paint the grass gray.

You'll find them in cafés . . .

waiting to play . . .

in boxes of toys . . .

or when things go astray.

Whenever you meet one, don't worry. Relax.
Take a deep breath and consider the facts.

Have a good look at it.

Call it by name.

(A Problem is sometimes quite easy to tame.)

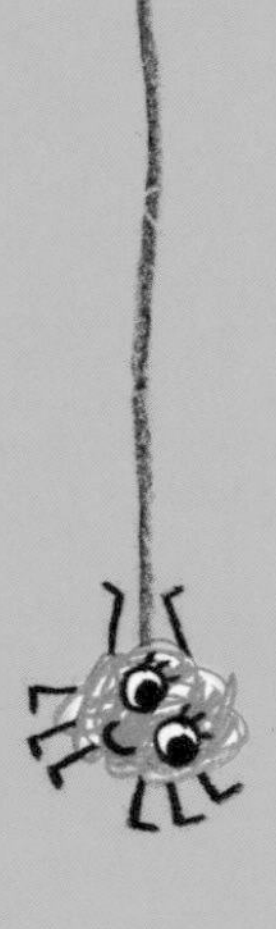

Look at it twice,
from a new point of view.

You're friendly,
actually.

Maybe it isn't a Problem for you.

The small ones annoy you
but often get bored.

They'll wander away when
they're being ignored.

Some need untangling. . . .

Some slowly fade. . . .

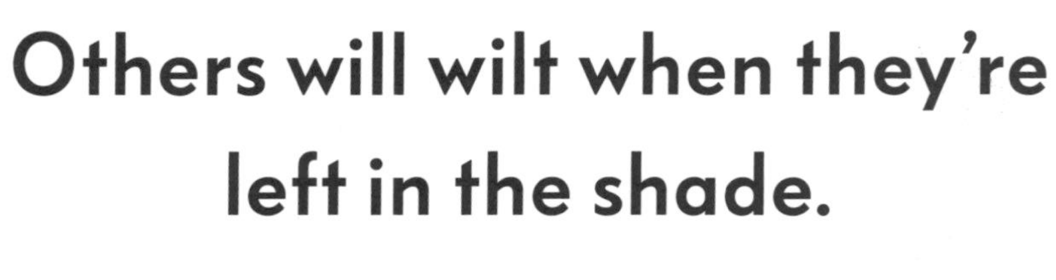

Others will wilt when they're left in the shade.

Problems breed Problems.
Please keep them apart.

Don't feed them.
Don't pet them.
Don't take them to heart.

If ever you spot one heading your way . . .
try to avoid it. Don't ask it to play.

Some you can sleep on.
They wake in the night,

then quietly tiptoe and slip from your sight.

But sometimes a Problem refuses to go.

And if that happens, it's handy to know . . .

Problems, like secrets,
are terribly shy. . . .

They hate to be shared.

So give it a try.

On a bench . . .

on a bus . . .

on a bed . . .

in an ear.

You'll feel much better. . . .

POP!
ZAP!

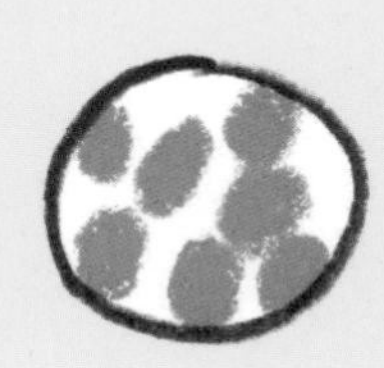

And they'll disappear.

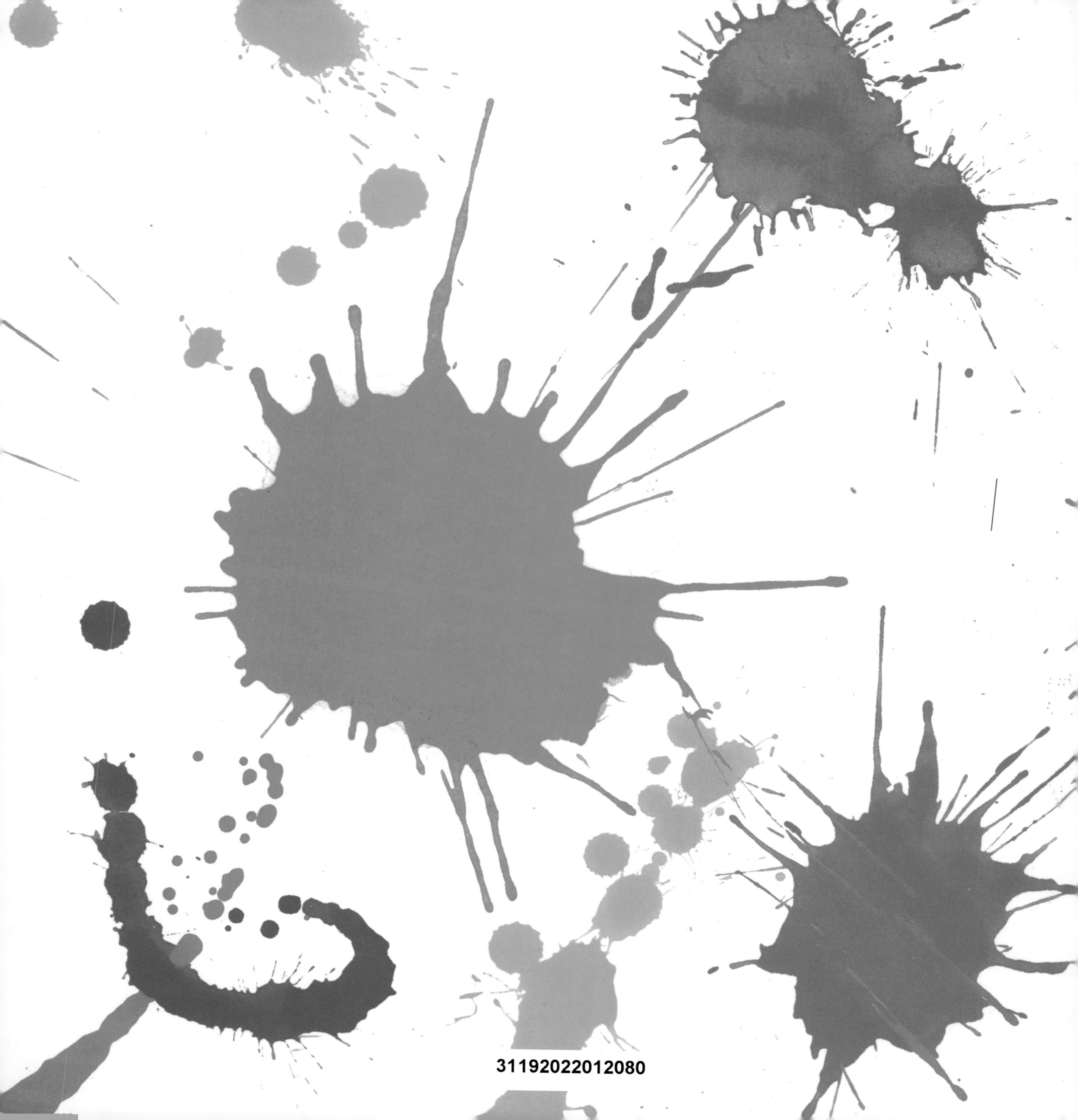